VALLEY OF DISASTER

The Johnstown Flood of 1889

Bonnie Highsmith Taylor

Perfection Learning®

Illustrations: Larassa Kabel

ABOUT THE AUTHOR

Bonnie Highsmith Taylor is a native
Oregonian. She loves camping in the Oregon
mountains and watching birds and other wildlife.
Writing is Ms. Taylor's first love. But she also
enjoys going to plays and concerts, collecting
antique dolls, and listening to good music.

Ms. Taylor is the author of several Animal
Adventures books, including *Lucy: A Virginia
Opossum* and *Zelda: A Little Brown Bat*. She
has also written novels, including *Gypsy in the
Cellar* and *Kodi's Mare*.

Image Credits: ArtToday (www.arttoday.com) pp. 38
(bottom), 54; Library of Congress pp. 6 (bottom), 9; NOAA
pp. 3, 38 (middle), 47, 52, 56; National Archives cover, p. 6
(top); National Park Service pp. 23, 38 (top), 53

For information, contact
Perfection Learning® Corporation
1000 North Second Avenue, P.O. Box 500,
Logan, Iowa 51546-0500.
Phone: 1-800-831-4190 • Fax: 1-712-644-2392
perfectionlearning.com

Paperback ISBN 0-7891-5638-5
Cover Craft® ISBN 0-7569-0613-x
2 3 4 5 6 7 PP 10 09 08 07 06 05

TABLE OF CONTENTS

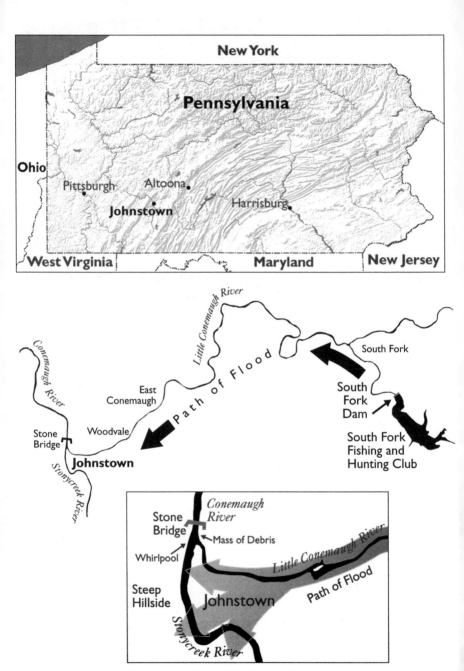

CHAPTER 1

Pa got up from the kitchen table. He poured himself another cup of coffee.

The Hales were eating breakfast late. It was a holiday—Decoration Day. There was no school, and the mill was closed.

In 1868, General John Logan, national commander of the Grand Army of the Republic,  declared May 30 as Decoration Day. This day was set aside to decorate the graves of soldiers killed in the Civil War.

Years later, the day was called Memorial Day. It honored those who died fighting in all wars.

In 1968, Congress passed a law making the last Monday in May a federal holiday honoring the war dead.

Pa finished his coffee. Then he walked to the window.

"Well, what do you know," said Pa. "The sun is shining."

Six-year-old Duane joined his father at the window. "It is!" he cried. "The sun is shining!"

Ma and Grandma began to clear the dishes from the table.

"I was beginning to think it would

never shine again, " Ma said. "Imagine, 100 days of rain or snow. And it's only the end of May."

Ben swallowed his last bite of oatmeal. He carried his bowl to the sink. Then he walked to the window.

The sun shone on the muddy water overflowing Stonycreek River.

Like everyone else, Ben was tired of the spring floods. Every year, it was the same. Stonycreek River and Conemaugh River overflowed. They flooded all the towns in the valley.

Grandma walked to the window. She put a hand on Ben's shoulder.

"Just look at that," she said. "The water is over the garden. All the plants will wash away."

"It happens nearly every year," Ma sighed. "We sometimes have to plant the garden twice."

Grandma shook her head. "I can't imagine why anyone would want to live in such a place."

"This is where Henry's work is," Ma reminded Grandma.

Mr. Hale didn't say anything. He worked at the Cambria Iron Mill. Nearly everyone in the valley towns worked at the mill.

Grandma was

> The Cambria Iron Mill was founded in 1852. It was one of the largest iron mills in the world. During the Civil War, the workers made cannons. Later, they made railroad tracks, wire, and other iron and steel products. At the time of the 1889 flood, the mill employed about 5,000 workers.

Ma's mother. She had come to live with the Hales two weeks before. She and Grandpa had lived in Altoona. But after Grandpa died, Ma asked her to move in.

Ben liked living in Johnstown. He didn't like the high waters that happened most springs. But they usually only lasted a short time.

Ben had lived his entire 11 years in Johnstown. He'd never wanted to live anywhere else.

Once when he was seven years old, Ben, Ma, Pa, and Duane had taken the train to Pittsburgh. Duane had been a baby.

The trip had been very exciting. And Ben had seen many interesting things.

Johnstown, Pennsylvania, was settled by a Swiss immigrant named Joseph Johns in 1793. Before then, it had been a Delaware Indian village.

Johnstown was built where Conemaugh River and Stonycreek River come together in a V. These creeks are very low during the summer. In fact, they can easily be waded across in places. But each spring, they overflow their banks.

But Ben didn't want to live there. He didn't even care for Altoona, where Grandma had lived. His family used to go there three or four times every year.

Ben didn't want to live anywhere but Johnstown. It was where his home and friends were.

Suddenly, Duane let out a big yell. "Hey! Now that it's quit raining, we can go to the parade."

"I don't know," said Ma. She looked at the sky. "It could start again any minute."

"If it does," Pa said, "we'll come home. I'd like to go to the cemetery too."

The cemetery was where Pa's brother was buried. He had died during the Civil War.

"Can we go to the parade?" Ben begged. "Please, Ma?"

Ma smiled. "It looks like we're going. Put on your rubber boots. We may have to wade all the way." Then she added, "Ben, you'll have to watch out for your little brother."

CHAPTER 2

The parade was wonderful. It was
the best one Johnstown had ever had.
Several bands marched and played.
They were Ben's favorite part.

Pa bought popcorn and lemonade for everyone. Then he went to the cemetery alone.

The rest of the family walked home. Duane ran ahead, whooping and hollering as always.

Ben thought how lucky Duane was. He had almost no chores to do. Ben had to split and carry the wood. He had to keep the porches swept. He had to empty the washtubs in the yard after Ma did laundry. He had to weed and water the garden all summer. And he always had to look out for Duane.

Before Grandma came, Ben and Duane had shared one of the upstairs bedrooms. Ma and Pa had the other one. But when Grandma arrived, Ben had to give up his bed.

Now Ben slept on a cot in the kitchen. Every morning, he had to fold the cot and put it away.

"Just be patient," Ma had said. "We hope it will only be for a short time. As soon as Pa gets his raise, we'll move into a bigger house. Then Grandma can have a room of her own."

By the time the family got home from the parade, Grandma was worn out.

"I believe I'll take a nap, Louise," she said to Ma. "Ben, help me up the stairs, please."

Ben let Grandma hold his arm while she climbed the stairs.

Even before Ben and Grandma were halfway up the stairs, Ma called. "Ben, cut me some kindling. I need to make a fire and cook supper."

After he left Grandma upstairs, Ben went to the woodshed. He saw about four inches of water covering the floor. It hadn't been there that morning.

Ben walked back to the house. He carried a load of kindling in his arms. It was hard to walk in the squishy mud.

Ben finally reached the porch. He worked his feet out of his boots. He walked into the kitchen in his stocking feet. Duane was on the floor playing with a magnet and a couple of nails.

"Water's in the woodshed, Ma," Ben said. "And it's halfway up to the porch."

"We'll start moving things upstairs," Ma said. "Just as soon as Pa gets home and we finish supper."

Every spring, the Hales had to move their belongings upstairs until the water went down.

"Just be happy we don't have carpets," Pa always said.

Ma always wanted carpets. Some of their neighbors had these huge rugs. They had to pull the tacks and try to get the carpets rolled up before water came into their houses. When the water went down, the neighbors carried the carpets downstairs again and retacked them.

When Pa got home from the cemetery, Ma had supper ready. She'd fixed fried chicken, mashed potatoes and gravy, and coleslaw. Grandma had baked two apple pies that morning.

Pa decided not to move things upstairs yet.

"The rain has let up," he said. "The waters may go back down."

Ma finally gave in. "Well—I hope we won't be sorry," she said.

Ben thought Pa could be right. It hadn't rained for most of the day. And he hated lugging all their stuff upstairs. Then he'd just have to carry it all back down again.

Ben cut more wood and filled the wood box. He swept the porches. Then he went next door to visit his best friend, Jess.

CHAPTER 3

By that night, it was raining again. Ben lay wide awake on his cot. He thought about what a good day it had been. Going to the parade and playing with Jess had been fun. Lucky Jess— he didn't have any little brothers or sisters.

Ben could hear the rain on the window getting louder. He had hoped it was nearly over.

School would be out in less than two weeks. Ben was looking forward to a dry summer vacation.

Ben fell asleep to the sound of the rain against the window. It beat harder and harder.

By morning, May 31, the water was up to the tops of the porches.

Ma was cooking thick slabs of bacon. Grandma was fixing scrambled eggs.

"Look at that nasty, dirty water," Grandma said. "It will be in the house in no time. What will you do then?"

"The same as we always do," Pa answered. "Go upstairs. It goes back down in a short time."

Ben wished Grandma would stop fussing. It made him nervous. And he could tell it upset Ma and Pa.

Ben loved his grandmother a lot. He remembered all the fun times visiting her and Grandpa in Altoona over the years. She always had something nice for him and Duane. Usually it was something she had made—knitted sweaters, hats, or scarves.

Ma packed Pa's lunch and he left for work. But in less than an hour, he returned.

"The mill is closed because of the high water," he said. "And school has been called off too."

The school was in an area even lower than the company houses where Ben lived.

Ben didn't mind missing school. But he knew he'd have to spend the day helping Pa move things upstairs. He would also have to listen to Grandma worry.

Ma began to pack towels, pictures, and sofa pillows. She packed everything the water might damage.

"We'll have to leave the kitchen table," Pa said. "It will be too hard to get up the stairs."

Ben carried up two kitchen chairs. Then he helped Pa carry up Ma's sewing machine.

There was a knock at the door. Duane opened it. Two young men who worked with Pa at the mill stood there. They were new to the town. Pa introduced them to the family.

One of the men said, "There's a lot of talk around town, Henry. They say the South Fork Dam is about to break."

Pa smiled. "They've been saying that for years, Ed. It hasn't broken yet."

"But there's been an awful lot of rain," Ed replied. "And they say the dam isn't kept in good repair."

Ben saw that Grandma had stopped what she was doing. She was listening to the men.

Pa glanced in her direction. Then he said, "I wouldn't worry, fellows. By tomorrow, the water will probably be back down. And that dam's as safe as can be."

But Ben knew better than that. He knew that Pa did too.

For a long time people had been worried about the safety of the dam. The lake and the land around it was owned by a hunting and fishing club. Pa had said lots of times that they should drain the lake and close the club.

VALLEY OF DISASTER

Year after year, rumors passed through town that the dam was going to break. But it never did.

The South Fork Dam was 14 miles east of Johnstown. The earthen dam had been built in 1849. Behind it was Lake Conemaugh. The lake was 3 miles long and 1 mile wide. In some places, it was 60 feet deep. The lake was 450 feet higher than Johnstown.

The dam had been built for a canal system. But after the railroads were built, the canals were no longer needed.

The dam and the surrounding land was bought by the South Fork Fishing and Hunting Club. Most of the members were wealthy businessmen, such as Andrew Carnegie, Andrew Mellon, and Henry Clay Frick.

It was well known that the dam was not kept in good repair. Many lawsuits were brought against the club after the dam broke. But it was decided that the flood was "an act of God." The flood had been caused by the unusual amount of rain. Therefore, the club was not responsible.

CHAPTER 4

Ben and Pa carried Ben's cot and bedding upstairs. Finally, they were finished moving things.

If the water entered the house, the family would go upstairs and wait out the flood.

"I've got some sewing I can do," Ma said.

Grandma had her knitting bag ready to take upstairs. "Well—well," she stammered. "If nobody else is— is worried, I guess I—I won't be either."

Ben could tell Grandma was scared to death. He felt sorry for her. He patted her arm. "We'll be all right, Grandma," he said.

Grandma smiled at Ben and squeezed his hand.

Pa filled the stove with wood. He closed the damper partway. "The upstairs will stay warm," he said. "At least through the day and part of the night."

Ben and Pa emptied the buckets from upstairs. They caught rainwater that came through the leaky roof.

By early afternoon, the Hale family was ready for the high water.

"I need a few things from the grocery store," Ma said

"Main Street is flooded," Pa replied. "The stores are probably closed. The shopkeepers were putting their goods on top shelves when I came through town this morning."

"Jack's Market may be open," Ma said. "It's up a little higher."

Pa finally gave in. Ma and Pa put on their boots.

Before they left, Ma said, "Ben, you watch your brother. Don't let him go outside."

Of course, thought Ben. Don't I always watch my little brother?

Ma and Pa left. Ben and Duane

watched them out the window. Ma was having a hard time keeping up with Pa. The water was up to her ankles.

The house seemed very quiet after Ma and Pa left. Grandma sat on a wooden stool. Her hands were folded on her lap.

"Do you want your knitting, Grandma?" Ben asked.

"No, thank you," Grandma answered in almost a whisper.

Duane sat on the floor. He was leafing through an old magazine. He hummed as he turned pages.

The only other sound was the roaring of the nearby creek. It was much louder than it had been earlier.

Ben hoped Ma and Pa wouldn't be gone long. The roaring of the creek was getting even louder.

"Grandma, Duane," Ben said. "I think it's time to go upstairs."

Ben held Grandma's arm as they climbed the stairs. He felt her trembling.

Duane ran ahead. He was whooping and hollering, as usual.

"Wow!" he cried, looking out the window. "Look how high it's getting."

Ben looked out the window. He looked down the stairs. Water was coming in under the back door.

"Oh, why don't Henry and Louise come back?" Grandma said as Ben helped her sit down.

"They'll be here soon, Grandma," Ben answered. But he was worried too.

Suddenly there was another sound. It nearly drowned out the roar of the water.

Grandma jumped up from her chair. "What on earth is that?" she cried.

"A train whistle," yelled Duane. "Ben, why is the train whistle blowing like that?"

For the first time, Duane looked frightened.

The whistle went on and on.

"What's wrong, Ben?" Duane cried.

Before Ben could answer, the whole house was shaken by a strong jolt. It was as though it had been struck by lightning. The sound of splitting timber filled the air.

Grandma's screams rang out, again and again.

Ben rushed to the window. His heart jumped to his throat at what he saw. A wall of water nearly as high as the house had hit them. Trees, logs, and lumber whirled about in the rushing water.

The dam! Ben thought wildly. The dam has broken!

Ben saw the roof of a shed go spinning by. Then an entire barn rushed past. It bounced at least three feet above the water. Then it came down with mighty splash. In a second, it was ripped to kindling.

"Ma! Pa!" Duane screamed.

The house was moving! It seemed impossible. But it was happening! It tipped to one side. Grandma fell to the floor, sobbing.

The house moved faster. Ben ran to the head of the stairs. Water was coming up toward him. Chairs and cupboards were floating on the water.

Duane was crying uncontrollably. Ma's words echoed in Ben's mind. "Take care of your brother."

But how? How? Ben wondered. How can I take care of any of us?

The house was struck by another jolt. Ben ran back to the window. As far as he could see was a sea of churning, muddy water. People were on top of buildings, whirling about on waves.

Ben's stomach lurched when he saw a human body facedown in the water.

Near the window, Ben saw what had jolted the house. It was a farm wagon. The tongue of the wagon was wedged between two boards on the side of the house. The boards had split apart. Ben watched the wagon bob up and down as the house moved.

Ben had an idea. But would it work?

He knew they had to get out of the house. In a short time, it would be full of water.

But the wagon tongue was wedged tightly. And the wagon was not directly under the window. They couldn't drop down into it.

Ben was frantic. How could he free the wagon? And how could they get in it before it floated away?

The harder Grandma and Duane screamed, the more frantic Ben grew. He looked around the room.

Don't panic, he tried to tell himself.

Then Ben saw a steel bed rail! It just might work. He could pry the wagon tongue free.

Ben pulled the bedding and mattress from Duane's bed. He got the rail loose.

The house was still moving. Ben fought to stay on his feet.

"Duane! Grandma!" he yelled. "Stand next to me! Do you hear me!"

Slowly, Ben's grandmother got to her feet. She staggered toward him. She pulled Duane by his arm.

Ben opened the window wide. The

water was even higher than before. Water splashed through the window.

It won't work, he thought. The wagon, when freed, would float away. They couldn't all get in it in time.

Ben would have to turn the wagon. He would have to free the jammed wagon tongue after they got on the wagon. If only they could do it.

Ben's heart pounded. He reached out the window. He held the rail tightly. The water whipped against it. The house moved on, pulling the wagon. Tighter and tighter Ben held the steel rail. It cut into his hands.

At last, he was able to wedge it between two spokes of one wagon wheel. He took a deep breath. His arms hurt from holding so tightly on the rail. But the wagon was moving. It moved slowly against the force of the water.

The next thing Ben knew, Grandma was leaning out of the window beside him. She grabbed hold of the rail. They both tugged as hard as they could. The wagon moved some more. At last, it was directly under the window.

"Climb out!" Ben shouted. "Hurry!"

Grandma went first.

"Come on, Duane! Now!"

Trembling, Duane put one leg over the windowsill. He fell into the bed of the wagon. Grandma reached for him.

Quickly, Ben threw the rail into the wagon. He tumbled out of the window. As he hit the wagon bed, the tongue broke loose.

Ben gave a huge sigh.

CHAPTER 5

Ben gasped for air. His heart
pounded in his ears.

One side of the wagon had been broken off. The front end was also broken. It was nearly ready to fall off.

"Hold on tight!" he screamed. "Don't let go! No matter what!"

Grandma was lying on her stomach. Her fingers were curled around the edge of the wagon bed. Her hands bled where the rail had cut into them.

Duane had his arms wrapped around Grandma's leg. He was not making a sound. But his whole body was shaking.

The wagon moved along in the dirty water. Suddenly, Ben heard a loud crash. He looked back.

Their house was being torn to pieces. Ben's eyes filled with tears. He couldn't believe what was happening. The only home he had ever known was gone. Homes all over town were being destroyed.

Something was moving in the water beside the wagon. It touched Ben's fingers as it brushed the wagon. It was a cow. Ben's throat tightened as he looked into the big, brown, frightened eyes. Ben heard the faint lowing. He closed his eyes.

The wagon seemed to be moving slower. The water was filled with debris—boards, tree limbs, furniture, stove pipes, pots and pans.

Ben choked back a sob when he thought of Ma and Pa. Would he ever see them again?

Ben couldn't stop the cry that came from his throat when he saw the body of a man tangled in the rubbish. It was someone he knew. Someone he had known all his life. He couldn't believe the horror. How could this be happening?

The bridge still stands today in the Johnstown Flood National Memorial.

The Pennsylvania Railroad Bridge was called the Stone Bridge. The bridge was five years old when the flood happened.

It had seven 58-foot-high spans, or arches. It had four railroad tracks, side by side. The bridge was 50 feet wide and was 32 feet above the waterline.

Duane lay so still and quiet. Ben shook him. Duane only groaned.

In every direction, Ben saw people on top of buildings. They screamed for help. But there was no way he could help them.

Ahead, Ben saw the old Stone Bridge. Debris was piled high. Telegraph poles zigzagged in the rubble.

Smoke was coming from the pile of debris. Then Ben saw flames.

How can there be fire in all this water? Ben wondered. Then it dawned on him. Some of the houses had had fires in the stoves. The fires had fallen out and spread.

The wagon was picking up speed. It had broken through some of the rubble.

Grandma slowly sat up. Duane's arms unwrapped from around her leg.

Duane curled up into a ball. He still made no sound.

Grandma's eyes were filled with tears. "We're going to die," she sobbed. "We're all going to die."

"Don't say that, Grandma," Ben pleaded. "Please don't say that."

The wagon bed picked up more speed. It began to turn around and around in the swirling water.

Then suddenly, the wagon struck a log. Grandma's scream pierced the air as she was thrown into the water. Ben made a desperate grab for her. He caught the skirt of her dress.

"Grandma! Grandma!" he shouted.

He held on tightly. He tried to reach her arm with his other hand. But it was no use. The swirling water pulled her away.

"Grandma!" he screamed again. He held a torn piece of cloth in his clenched fist.

He threw himself face down. He cried until his throat hurt. Duane did not move. He did not make a sound. He lay on his side curled in a tight ball.

Ben held fast to the edge of the wagon. Once more, the wagon slowed down. Ahead, Ben saw that the flames at the bridge had spread. They were shooting higher. If the wagon rammed into the rubble, it would catch fire.

About six feet to the side of the wagon, the debris looked as if it was packed solid.

If they could reach the pile, maybe they could walk across it. Then maybe they could reach dry land. Otherwise, they would soon be in the fire.

Ben shook his brother. "Duane!" he shouted. "Get up!"

Duane raised his head. His jaw was quivering. "Ma, Pa," he whispered.

Ben shook Duane's shoulders hard. "Listen to me," he said. "We have to get off! Now!"

Duane stared into space.

Ben knew there was not much time. The wagon bed bumped against the jam of logs and brush. He could only hope that the rubble was solid.

He pulled Duane to the edge of the wagon bed. Ben staggered to his feet. He fought to keep his balance. He took a deep, deep breath. Then, he jumped. He landed on his knees. The rubble splashed in the water.

Ben turned toward Duane. "Duane! Jump!" he called.

Duane sat still staring into space.

Ben stood up. His legs wobbled.

"Do you hear me, Duane!" he yelled. "Jump!"

Still the boy sat, staring.

"Okay, stay!" Ben shouted. "Just

stay. I'm leaving!"

He turned, as though to walk away.

"Ben!" Duane's high scream pierced the air. "Wait!"

Ben moved as close to the edge of the debris as he dared.

"Okay, now jump!"

Duane got to his feet. "I—I can't. I—I'm afraid."

"Either jump or be burned to death," Ben hollered.

Duane looked toward the burning rubble at the bridge.

He started crying. "I'll—I'll jump, Ben. I will." Then he whimpered. "Don't let me die, Ben. Please don't let me die."

Duane stood wobbling for several seconds. At last, he jumped. But he landed in the water. Ben reached down for him. He couldn't reach him.

Ben hurriedly picked up a long limb from the jam. He held it out. Finally, Duane closed his hands around the limb. Slowly, Ben pulled him out of the water.

Duane threw himself into Ben's arms. He was trembling and sobbing.

Ben held Duane close to him. He had never loved his little brother so much.

CHAPTER 6

That night, Ben and Duane lay on
the pile of wet debris. Duane slept.
But he sobbed and trembled all night.

The night air was filled with screams and cries of humans and animals. Dogs howled. Cows lowed as they struggled in the water.

Over and over, Ben saw his grandmother slipping from his grasp. He felt so bad. He would sleep on a cot forever if he could only have her back.

He thought of Ma and Pa. What would happen to him and his brother if they were dead?

He was afraid to go to sleep. What if the rubble broke free and floated away? What if they both fell into the water?

At last, Ben slept. He was wakened by voices nearby. He raised up. Two men were coming towards the boys. Ben knew one of the men. It was someone Pa worked with.

"Is that you, Ben?" he called. "Henry Hale's boy?"

"Yes, sir," Ben answered. "Have you seen my mother and father? Do you know if they're okay?"

"Let's go find out," the man answered.

The man picked Duane up and carried him. Once more, Duane seemed to be in a daze. Ben followed the men across the logjam. They moved very slowly.

Ben shuddered at the sights they passed. The fire at the bridge still smoldered. Dead animals floated on top of the water. Rats ran everywhere. Rescue crews were carrying people on stretchers.

The official count of deaths was 2,209. Almost 1,000 bodies were never found. The fire at Stone Bridge was responsible for about 300 of those deaths.

Over 1,500 homes were destroyed. Property damage totaled about $17 million.

Some people were injured. Many were dead. Very few buildings were still standing.

After about an hour, Ben and the others reached their destination. A refugee camp and hospital had been set up. It was in a flat spot about 200 feet above the flooded area. Large tents served as hospitals. Smaller tents were for the people who were homeless.

Hundreds of people milled around the area. Some people were putting up more tents. More and more people were arriving.

A nurse took Duane from the arms of the man who had carried him.

"I think he may be in shock," she said. "He'll be all right in a little while."

She carried him into a large tent.

The man said, "Come on, Ben. Let's look for your folks."

They walked around and around the camp. Ben saw a lot of people he knew. But there was no sign of his mother or father.

Ben walked back to the hospital tent. He sat down on the ground.

"I'll just stay here," he told the man. "I'll wait and see how my brother is."

The man squeezed Ben's arm and walked off.

Ben was so tired. He lay down and put his head on his arm. There was so much noise. Everyone seemed to be calling for someone. A lot of people were crying.

Ben dozed off.

"Ben. Oh, Ben," a voice called, coming nearer.

Ben opened his eyes. In less than a moment, he was in his mother's arms. They were both crying.

Ben told Ma about Grandma. He told her Duane was okay, and he was being cared for.

Then Ben asked, "Where's Pa? Is— is he all right?"

"I'll take you to see him," Ma answered.

She led him to a tent. A lot of injured people lay on cots. Pa was in the back. Ben hardly recognized him. His head was wrapped in a bandage. One arm was in a sling.

"We tried to get back home," Pa said. "We hunted for you and Duane."

"Your father was injured rescuing a woman and her baby from the floodwater," Ma said.

Ben told Ma and Pa everything that had happened. His voice quivered when he talked about Grandma.

"I tried so hard," he whispered. "But—but I couldn't save her."

"You did a fine job, son," Pa said. "We're very proud of you."

Ma smiled and gave Ben a big hug. "And you took such good care of your little brother," she said.

AFTERWORD

All through the early morning hours of May 31, 1889, men worked tirelessly to save the South Fork Dam. They dug trenches to drain some of the water from the lake. They added more dirt to the top of the dam.

At 11:30 a.m., Elias Unger, the South Fork Fishing and Hunting Club president, realized the dam probably could not be saved. He sent John Parke, Jr., the dam's engineer, to South Fork to warn the people there. Parke also sent telegraph warnings to Johnstown.

Many Johnstown residents felt there was no danger. They had heard these warnings for years. The creeks and rivers in the area always flooded the town in the spring.

But at 3:10 p.m., the dam finally gave way. About 20 million tons of water crashed down the valley toward Johnstown. The wall of water reached 60 feet tall at times. It moved through the town at 40 miles an hour, leveling everything in its path.

A few days after the flood, Clara Barton and the newly organized American Red Cross arrived. Barton had been a nurse during the Civil War. In 1881, she founded the American Red Cross.

The Red Cross had helped in other disasters. But none had been as bad as the Johnstown flood.

Fifty doctors and nurses came with Barton. They set up hospitals in tents. Clara Barton herself worked around the clock. She was responsible for collecting thousands of dollars' worth of clothing, blankets, and food. She said that she would stay as long as she was needed. She stayed for five months.

Donations of money and supplies came from everywhere. Andrew

Carnegie donated enough money to build a library in Johnstown. Other members of the South Fork Fishing and Hunting Club donated thousands of dollars for the relief effort.

Even the lord mayor of Dublin, Ireland, and the sultan of Turkey sent money to the people of Johnstown.

It took five years for Johnstown to fully recover.

A flood in 1936 killed 25 people. It caused $40 million in property damage. In 1937, a flood-control system was built.

A 1977 flood killed 85 people. This flood caused more than $300 million in damages.

About 70 years before the flood of 1889, floodwaters sent thousands of pumpkins from farm fields through the streets of Johnstown. This was called the Pumpkin Flood.

Today, the Johnstown Flood
National Memorial is located about 10
miles from Johnstown. The park
covers about 165 acres and contains
the remains of the South Fork Dam.